John Ruskin in his room at No. 28 Herne Hill, c. 1886

JOHN RUSKIN'S CAMBERWELL

James S. Dearden

Published for
THE GUILD OF ST GEORGE
by
BRENTHAM PRESS

First published 1990 by Brentham Press
40 Oswald Road, St Albans, Herts AL1 3AQ

GUILD OF ST GEORGE
Secretary: Mr J. P. Cordery
Hope Orchard, Castlemorton, Malvern, Worcs WR13 6JB

British Library Cataloguing in Publication Data
Dearden, James S. (James Shackley)
John Ruskin's Camberwell.
1. English literature. Ruskin, John 1819–1900. Local associations. (London Borough). Southwark Camberwell
I. Title
828.809

ISBN 0-905772-26-1

Printed in Great Britain by
Headley Brothers Limited, Invicta Press, Ashford, Kent and London.

Contents

To my granddaughter
HARRIET LUCY WASHINGTON

Acknowledgements

During the preparation of this book I have received help from many quarters, and I am very grateful to all of those who have patiently answered my questions. Particularly I should like to thank Charles Fyffe, who first introduced me to Ruskin's Camberwell, and who later returned there with me to take some of the photographs which are reproduced here. I am also particularly grateful to Alan Doe, Head of the Geography Department at Bembridge School, Isle of Wight, for preparing the map for me. Stephen Humphreys of the Southwark Local Studies Library has been an invaluable and patient mine of local knowledge, and I am very grateful to him for all his help.

For permission to reproduce material in their collections I am indebted to the owners who are acknowledged in the List of Illustrations.

To Anthony Harris, Master of the Guild of St George, I am grateful for the idea which began this book, and for the suggestion that it should be published by the Guild.

J.S.D.

List of Illustrations

MAP OF CAMBERWELL

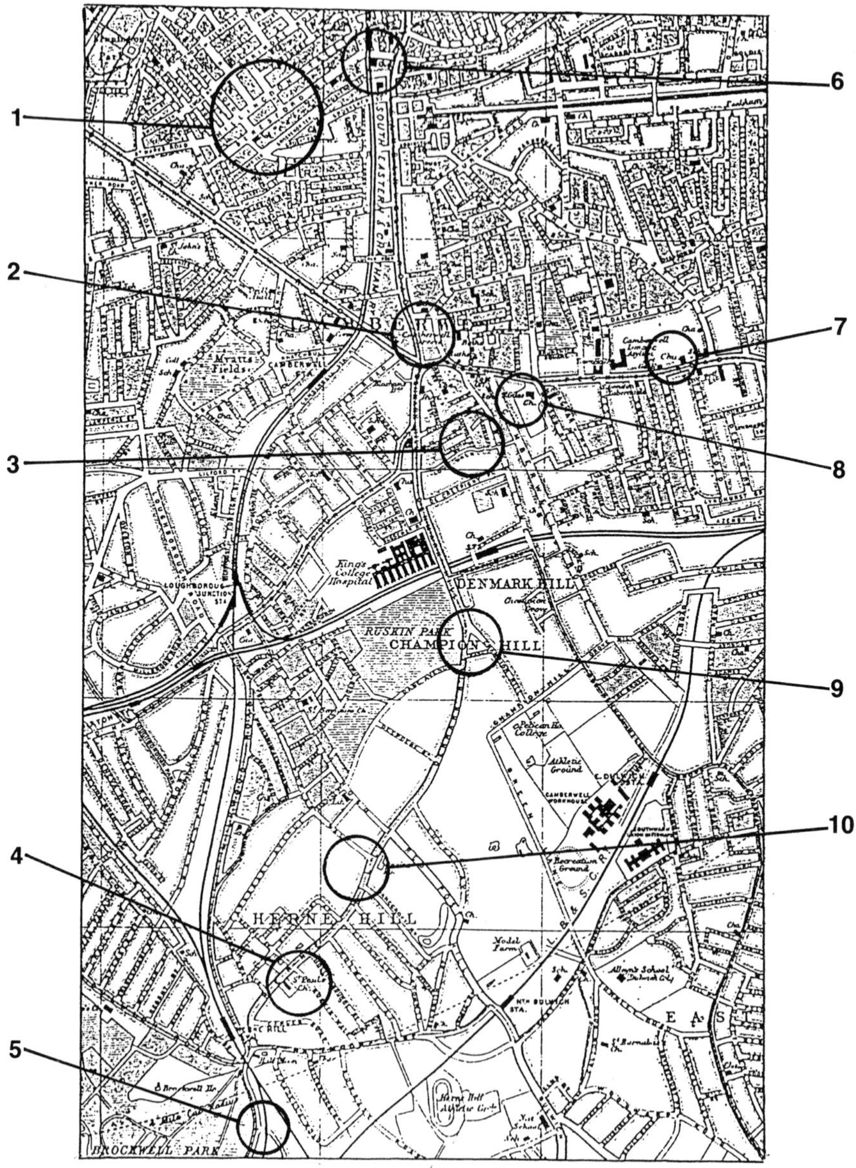

1. Beresford Street, now John Ruskin Street; 2. Camberwell Green; 3. Grove Lane and Camberwell Hall; 4. St Paul's Church; 5. Croxted Lane; 6. Beresford Chapel; 7. Camden Chapel; 8. St Giles Church; 9. 163 Denmark Hill; 10. 28 Herne Hill

1 Ruskin and Camberwell

Although John Ruskin was born in Hunter Street, Brunswick Square, on 8 February 1819, he had long and important association with Camberwell which was his home until he was fifty-two years old.

His parents, John James and Margaret Ruskin, were first cousins and on their marriage in 1818 they had settled in a terraced house in Hunter Street. John James was the active partner in the sherry importing firm of Ruskin, Telford and Domecq, which had been established just a few years earlier. He was an astute businessman and as the agent for the leading exporters of sherry from Jerez, he was, through much hard work, busily making his fortune. As he became more and more successful, he and his family moved to larger houses in more desirable surroundings, first to a semi-detached house in Herne Hill, and then to a detached house standing in its own grounds on Denmark Hill.

John Ruskin himself remembered little of the house where he was born, except watching the water cart being filled in Hunter Street, the coal men filling the cellar through the hole in the pavement, and the dust men clearing out the ash hole. But even at that early age he had an inquiring mind and remembered examining the knots in the wood of his nursery floor, and counting the bricks of the houses across the street.

His association with south London began in these first three and a half years of his life, while the family still lived in Hunter Street. In the first chapter of his autobiography *Praeterita,*[1] Ruskin remembered 'for a few weeks in the summer breathing country air by taking lodgings in small cottages (real cottages, not villas, so-called) either about Hampstead, or at Dulwich, at "Mrs Ridley's", the last of a row in a lane which led out into the Dulwich fields . . .'

When John James decided that his business had prospered sufficiently to allow him to move with his family to a respectable distance out of the smell and bustle of London, perhaps it was *his* recollections of Mrs Ridley's cottage that led him to Camberwell.

In March 1823 the Ruskins took No 28 Herne Hill, one of two pairs of semi-detached houses right on the top of Herne Hill. The four-storeyed house commanded extensive views of the countryside for miles around. There was a front garden filled with evergreens, lilac and laburnum, and a long, narrow, back garden where there was an old mulberry tree, cherry trees, blackcurrant and gooseberry bushes. The pear and apple trees—the envy of Herne Hill—had been planted by the Ruskins' predecessor, Mr John Jones, a linen draper of Cheapside.

Remembering little of Hunter Street, 28 Herne Hill became Ruskin's *real* home, where his formative years were spent. This was what he remembered as stability, and where he grew up. This was where he came home from school, and later, from university. Here his early writing was done—the early poems and geological articles, 'The Poetry of Architecture' in Loudon's *Architectural Magazine,* and the first volume of *Modern Painters*, the book which was to bring him fame and power in Victorian England.

The Ruskins lived here for nearly twenty years. By now, John James's income was substantial and his son was well known. They had outgrown their semi-detached house on Herne Hill and needed somewhere a little more befitting their station. In October 1842 they moved a little nearer to London, to No 163 Denmark Hill, a substantial house on the eastern side of the road, now opposite to Ruskin Park. The Denmark Hill house stood in some seven acres of ground, and was approached by its carriage drive which ran from the lodge at the gate, in a sweeping curve flanked by evergreens, to the porticoed front door.

Behind was a meadow, and outbuildings, upper and lower kitchen gardens, an orchard, and wooded walks. The house itself was large and expensive to run; a large staff was required.

But Ruskin was never really happy here; it was not *home* to him. At the time of the move, John James was 57 and his wife 61. Increasingly Ruskin felt the responsibility of his gradually ageing parents. Although the Ruskins were inveterate travellers, it was not until 1845 that John visited the continent without his parents. And when he did, they missed him a great deal, and he felt guilty about being away from them.

During John's short-lived marriage to Effie Gray, much of their time was spent abroad. But for a while 163 Denmark Hill was their home, and later they set up house at 30 Herne Hill.

Following his marriage Ruskin spent much time travelling, either in this country or on the continent. Yet more and more, when he was away from home, he was beset by a feeling of guilt at leaving his parents, knowing that they were missing him and worrying about his welfare. And when he was at home, there was always an uncomfortableness; no sooner had Ruskin returned to Denmark Hill, than he wanted to be away again, and indeed he contemplated settling in Switzerland.

In 1864 John James Ruskin died, leaving John to inherit all of his property, valued at some £160,000. A distant cousin, Joan Agnew, came to live at Denmark Hill as companion to his widow who lived on until the end of 1871. A few months earlier her son, now Slade Professor of Fine Art at Oxford, had bought Brantwood, a house of his own on the eastern shore of Coniston Lake, in the Lake District. He was also about to acquire rooms at Corpus Christi College, Oxford. The remaining lease of Denmark Hill was sold to Mr Walter Druce. Meanwhile, Joan Agnew had married Arthur Severn, a watercolour artist and son of Joseph Severn, the friend of Keats, in the summer of 1871. John James had retained the lease of 28 Herne Hill when the

1a *Margaret Ruskin*

1b *John James Ruskin*

2a *Joan Severn*

2b *Arthur Severn*

family moved to the Denmark Hill house in 1842, and in 1871 Ruskin gave the remainder of the lease to the Severns as a wedding present.

Brantwood now became Ruskin's home and increasingly ill-health curtailed his travelling. The last time he was at Herne Hill was in December 1888. He had returned, a sick man, from his final visit to France, Switzerland and Italy and stayed at 28 Herne Hill from 9 to 29 December. He had six more active months left to him. Then illness kept him at Brantwood for the remaining eleven years of his life. He died there in January 1900.

*

The appearance of the first volume of *Modern Painters* in 1843 laid the foundations of Ruskin's career as an art critic. The book had grown out of an earlier defence of J.M.W. Turner which he had written. His admiration for Turner's work had led the Ruskins, father and son, to collect Turner's watercolours; later Ruskin was to become Turner's executor and be the first to sort and catalogue Turner's bequest to the nation. *Modern Painters* went on for four more volumes, the final one eventually appearing in 1860.

Meanwhile, from Ruskin's love of gothic architecture had come *The Poetry of Architecture,* and the three volumes of *The Stones of Venice.* In one of the chapters in the latter, 'On the nature of gothic architecture', Ruskin considered the lot of the medieval craftsman. It was a short step to an examination of the role of the contemporary artist and the debt owed to him by society, and to a questioning and re-examination of the whole Victorian structure of social and political economy.

Out of respect for his father's views, Ruskin was not too outspoken. However, following his father's death in 1864 he felt free to express his own views on the injustices of the time, and while his career as a writer and lecturer on art continued, his writings on social and political economy developed with such books as *Unto this Last* and *Crown of Wild Olive.*

Ruskin was one of the most prolific of nineteenth-century writers. Throughout a long and active career he had taught the dignity of labour and extolled the beauty of gothic architecture. He had championed the Pre-Raphaelites and introduced the English to Tintoretto and other early Italian artists. William Morris, Bernard Shaw, Marcel Proust, Mahatma Gandhi all considered his teaching of great importance. Most of the early English socialists acknowledged their debt to him; in America a town called Ruskin was established where a small community practised what Ruskin had preached. Meanwhile in England, his Utopian Guild of St George sought to establish a community where life was fair and the Companions found happiness and satisfaction through work with their hands. The Guild still continues to champion causes which it believes Ruskin would approve.

Elsewhere the effects of his teaching can be seen today in green belts around city sprawl, smokeless zones, fair rents, town planning and the National Trust. Ruskin was truly one of the great figures of the nineteenth century, whose influence is still very much with us.

3 No. 28 Herne Hill

2 No. 28 Herne Hill

'When I was about four years old', Ruskin wrote in *Praeterita*,[2] 'my father found himself able to buy the lease of a house on Herne Hill, a rustic eminence four miles south of the "Standard" in Cornhill', the water conduit at the east end of Cornhill from which distances from London were officially measured.

Herne Hill at that time was becoming a fashionable suburb and the country road running south from Camberwell was discreetly flanked by the beginnings of a ribbon development of large semi-detached houses. No 28 Herne Hill, to which the Ruskins moved in March 1823 was one of two pairs of semi-detached houses on the top of the hill.

The house occupied a plot of land approximately 110 yards long by 16 yards wide. The front garden had its tree-flanked drive where, Ruskin tells us, his mother enjoyed tending lilacs and laburnums. The house was set some 30 yards back from the road. Behind the house, the garden stretched for a further 67 yards, and as has already been described, was filled with old-established fruit trees, the envy of Herne Hill; but to the young Ruskin, 'an Eden where all the fruit was forbidden'.[3] From the upper of the four floors of the house were views of St Paul's and Greenwich, of the Norwood hills on one side and the Thames valley on the other, 'with Windsor telescopically clear in the distance, and Harrow, conspicuous always in fine weather to open vision against the summer sunset'.[4]

The houses on Herne Hill were leasehold, the lease of No 28 being owned at that time by T. J. Moores. From 1823 when they moved to Herne Hill, until 1829, John James Ruskin rented the house from Mr Moores, not buying the lease from him until 1829. In that year he paid £2227 12s. for the lease which ran until 1887.

Precisely how big the house was at that time is not easy to determine. Almost certainly it would have been larger than the house in Hunter Street from which they had moved; that had eleven rooms on four floors, together with several rooms in the basement and a three or four roomed servants' cottage in the yard at the back.

I know of no description of 28 Herne Hill to indicate the layout of its interior. We can tell from views of the front of the house that there was a semi-basement with four floors above. The only plan[5] that I know shows that the front door, approached by a flight of seven steps, opened into an entrance hall, of which the further end was occupied by the staircase. To the left, by 1900, was one large room with two windows looking over the front garden and French windows at the other end leading to the garden at the back. Originally this room had probably been two. The part of the house to the right of the hall presents a problem. In the Ruskin and Arthur Severn drawings of the front of the house there are what appear to be coach-house doors to

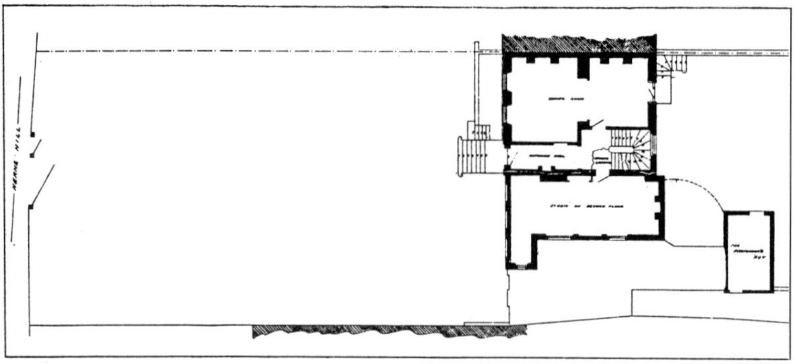

4 Plan of No. 28 Herne Hill

the right of the front door, and in the 1900 plan this area is marked 'Studio on second floor'. The Ruskins do not appear to have kept a carriage when they lived at Herne Hill, so what this part was used for at that time is doubtful.

Some indication of the number of rooms in the house may come from an examination of the number of people living there. In 1827 there were John James and Margaret Ruskin; John, with his bedroom in the attic; and one male and three female members of staff. A year later Mary Richardson, the orphaned daughter of John James's sister and her husband, joined the family. She was four years older than John and she lived with the Ruskins for the next nineteen years, until her marriage. By 1830 the staff situation had changed; the man Thomas had left at the beginning of the year and two extra female servants were taken on, making five female staff in all. (By 1842 John's manservant 'George' had been added to the five females.) Additionally there was room in the house for visitors, but facilities must have been somewhat stretched when Pedro Domecq and his four daughters came to stay in 1836! 'How we got them all into Herne Hill corners and cupboards', wrote Ruskin in *Praeterita*,[6] 'would be inexplicable without a plan of the three stories! The arrangements were half Noah's ark, half Doll's house, but we got them all in'.

The advent of Mary Richardson in 1828 and the purchase of the lease in 1829 made John James decide on extensions to his house. These were carried out in 1830–1. We do not know exactly what they comprised, but building and furnishing the extension cost a little over £2000—so when one recalls that the 58 years' lease had cost £2227, the £2000 extension must have been substantial. Perhaps the two floors above the 'coach house' were added at this time.

We only know the specific location of two rooms in the house. Ruskin's nursery, and later his bedroom, was the room at the front of the house with the arched top window on the very top floor. Later, his

5 No. 28 Herne Hill from back

study was on the floor below—in the front view of the house, the window directly below his nursery and the window to the left.

It was in these rooms, and probably in his little niche in the drawing room, where Ruskin's earliest literary work was done. His 'first letter' to his father (written by his mother at his dictation, but bearing his first signature) is dated 15 March 1823; it was written either *just* before they left Hunter Street, or *just* after they moved into Herne Hill. His juvenile poetry was written here. Hence would have been borne with pride *The Spiritual Times* in February 1830 containing his first publications, the poems 'Skiddaw' and 'Derwent Water'; Loudon's *Magazine of Natural History* of 1834 and 1836 with his early essays; the *Architectural Magazine* of 1837–8 with his 'Poetry of Architecture' essays; the annuals with his later poems, *Salsette and Elephanta*, his first work to have independent existence. And here the planning and almost certainly some of the writing took place of his first great work, the first volume of *Modern Painters*.

> I well remember my father's rushing up to the drawing-room at Herne Hill, with wet and flashing eyes, with the proof in his hand of the first sentences of his son's writing ever set in type . . . My mother and I eagerly questioning the cause of his excitement,—'It's—it's only *print*', said he'![7]

But it was the outside of the house, the gardens, which Ruskin chiefly remembered. While his father was at his office in Billiter Street, the young Ruskin watched his mother working in the garden. His first joy of the year was the snowdrops and the second cardinal one the almond blossom. His chief pleasure of the fruit tree avenue was its blossom, not its fruit. The first gooseberries of the year were picked for John James's birthday on 10 May—then the family was free to accompany John James on his business journey in Britain or later to embark on their continental tours.

At the far end of the garden was the stable. Here in 1829 lived Shagram, Ruskin's Shetland pony. The ten year-old Ruskin had been taking lessons at a riding school in Moorfields—which he hated. Then his parents bought Shagram, on which he was dragged around the Norwood lanes on a leading rein. On his return home he was so questioned about his performance that he became more and more nervous after each tumble. Eventually this branch of his education was abandoned, and presumably Shagram was sold.

It was also to the stable, perhaps very soon after they moved to Herne Hill, that young John was carried, for safety by their manservant Thomas, to see Lion, the black Newfoundland guard dog which they had on trial. Lion was eating, and when Thomas bent down so that Ruskin could see him better, Lion jumped up and bit John's lip. Stitches were needed and slight lifelong disfigurement remained. Lion had to go, but Ruskin's love of dogs remained. Over the years he had bulldogs, St Bernards, collies. Perhaps their earliest dog was the King Charles spaniel to be seen in the 1822 portrait of Ruskin by

Northcote. Perhaps Lion was replaced by Gypsy, a dog which they owned in early 1829. About this time they acquired Dash, the brown and white spaniel which had belonged to Bridget Richardson, Ruskin's Croydon aunt. Dash was with them till he died ten years later, in 1839, to be immediately replaced by Cyrus, who was still with the family three years later. By about 1843 Tug had appeared on the scene, and about 1849 there was Mungo. Between 1852 and 1858—after the Herne Hill days—Ruskin owned Wisie, the Spitz which he was given in Venice by Count Thun and after an adventurous journey came back home and 'became a bright part of my mother's day as well as mine . . .'[8]

Ruskin described his childhood afternoons in his autobiography:

> In the afternoons, when my father returned (always punctually) from his business, he dined, at half-past four, in the front parlour, my mother sitting beside him to hear the events of the day, and give counsel and encouragement with respect to the same;—chiefly the last, for my father was apt to be vexed if orders for sherry fell the least short of their due standard, even for a day or two. I was never present at this time, however, and only avouch what I say by hearsay and probable conjecture; for between four and six it would have been a grave misdemeanour in me if I so much as approached the parlour door. After that, in summer time, we were all in the garden as long as the day lasted; tea under the white-heart cherry tree; or in winter or rough weather, at six o'clock in the drawing-room,—I having my cup of milk, and slice of bread-and-butter, in a little recess, with a table in front of it, wholly sacred to me; and in which I remained in the evenings as an Idol in a niche, while my mother knitted, and my father read to her,—and to me, so far as I chose to listen.[9]

It was while they lived at Herne Hill that the Ruskins were able to lay the foundations of their art collection. John's interest in Prout and Turner stemmed from the 1832 gift to him of Rogers's *Italy* and the purchase of Prout's *Sketches in Flanders and Germany*. Their first Turner watercolour, of Richmond in Surrey, was bought in January 1839. By the time they left the house in 1842 they had ten Turner watercolours adorning their walls, including Winchelsea, Coblentz and Lucerne. They also had nine works by Prout, as well as examples by Cattermole, Clarkson Stanfield, Cox, Harding, Roberts, Copley Fielding, Holland and others.

The Ruskins entertained regularly. Guests, such as the Domecqs or Scottish friends, came to stay, or those from closer at hand, such as Samuel Prout, Osborne Gordon, the Grays, James Hogg, the 'Ettrick Shepherd', the Rev. George Croly, Rector of St Stephen's, Walbrook, and W. H. Harrison, editor of *Friendship's Offering* and Ruskin's literary mentor.

For some years now Ruskin, Telford and Domecq had headed the list of sherry shippers from Jerez with about 2000 butts annually, and the business was thriving. By 1842 John had reached maturity, graduated from Oxford, and was writing his first great book. An era

6 Interior at No. 28 Herne Hill

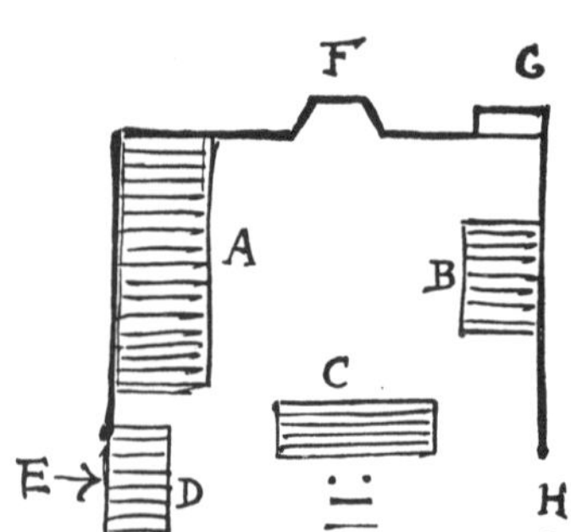

7 Ruskin's plan of his Herne Hill bedroom

8 Ruskin's nursery, later his bedroom, at No. 28 Herne Hill

was ending and the Ruskins were looking for a new and larger home, more befitting their improved station in life.

In October 1842 they moved from 28 Herne Hill to the much larger 163 Denmark Hill. But that was not the end of the Herne Hill house in the Ruskin story. John James retained the lease, and let the house (for £116 p.a.) to a Miss Sarah Lee. At some stage, E. T. Cook says in *Homes and Haunts of John Ruskin*[10] that Ruskin used the house as a kind of museum for his geological and other collections. On the death of his father in 1864 Ruskin inherited the property and from 1871 28 Herne Hill became the home of Joan and Arthur Severn.

This time coincided with the death of Margaret Ruskin, the closing of the Denmark Hill house and the removal of Ruskin to rooms in Oxford and to his new home of Brantwood at Coniston. He had a need for a London base, and the Severns put his old nursery at the top of their new home at his permanent disposal. He used the room frequently during the next eighteen years.

The room was painted by Arthur Severn, and Ruskin's portrait by Blake Wirgman, made there, shows some of the room. Ruskin described the room in a letter to Susan Beever[11] about 1882:

> The little room, which I think, is as nearly as possible the size of your study, but with a lower roof, has to begin with—A, my bed; B, my basin stand; C, my table; D, my chest of drawers; thus arranged in relation to E, the window (which still has its dark bars to prevent the little boy getting out); F, the fireplace; G, the golden or mineralogical cupboard; and H, the grand entrance. The two dots with a back represent my chair, which is properly solid and not un-easy. Three others of lighter disposition find

place somewhere about. These with the chimney-piece and drawer's head are covered, or rather heaped, with all they can carry . . . The chimney-piece with its bottles, spoons, lozenge boxes, matches, candlesticks, and letters jammed behind them, does appear to me entirely hopeless . . .

In this room substantial parts of some of Ruskin's later books were written; indeed, the preface for his autobiography was dated from here in 1885.

The lease of the house had expired in 1887 and Arthur Severn renewed it for a further 21 years. At the time of Ruskin's death in 1900 the Ruskin Union's Memorial Committee examined the possibility of taking over the house and establishing it as a Ruskin Museum and Settlement. But nothing came of the proposal and it remained the Severns' London home until the new lease expired in September 1907. They then leased 9 Warwick Square in Victoria, and Joan wrote of their old home, 'I suppose they will pull it down before long and build horrid little houses like those with which it is now surrounded—and all the old associations and beauty of the place, be swept away'.[12]

When E. T. Cook visited the house in 1912 the distant views had been built out, the glories of the garden remained but the house was much dilapidated, and it was soon pulled down. A memorial post was subsequently placed in the garden of the new house on its site.

9 The garden at No. 28 Herne Hill

3 No. 163 Denmark Hill

In the early 1840s the Ruskins' situation had reached the stage where they were looking for a larger and more suitable house. In October 1841 John James Ruskin had written to his son, 'Mama seems so sick of Herne Hill present House that we must move.'[13] In fact in August John James had told his son, 'we are on the lookout for a House *not* in Town'.[14] They looked at a house in Tooting, but it was too far 'out of the way'. They were in treaty with a publisher, Mr Tegg, for his house with its 25 acres. But Margaret Ruskin didn't like its situation. They had looked at the house in Fulham belonging to the Gunters—'a good house but in a horrid corner all kitchen gardens and manure'.[15] In October they had offered £4800 for the lease of a house on Denmark Hill, but the offer was refused.

However, negotiations continued and in October of the following year John James Ruskin paid £4800 for the remaining 36 years' lease of No. 163 Denmark Hill. He paid a further £1059 for the fixtures which he listed in his account book— 'carpets glasses window laths cornices curtains fenders floor cloths part drawing room furniture and other things not fixed. Iron fencing, summer houses, erections in green houses, garden implements, pump, hay, tank, garden lights, plants, manure, brewing utensils.'

The new house was some three-quarters of a mile north west of the Herne Hill house, nearer Camberwell. The Ruskins would have passed its gates, near the junction of Denmark Hill and Champion Hill, whenever they went into Camberwell or London. With its own lodge, the new house stood in seven acres of ground. There were gardens, orchards, glasshouses, a field, and extensive outbuildings.

'My mother did like arranging the rows of pots in the big greenhouse', wrote Ruskin in *Praeterita,* 'and we bought three cows, and skimmed our own cream, and churned our own butter. And there was a stable, and a farmyard, and a haystack, and a pigstye, and a porter's lodge, where undesirable visitors could be stopped before startling us with a knock.'[16]

The house itself was substantial. The centre block had three floors and basements; wings extended at both sides. In front, the columns and portico in the centre had a large window above them on each floor; to left and to right there were two windows on each floor. On the lawn across the carriage drive was a big cedar tree. At the back 'the view from the breakfast room into the field was really very lovely'.[17] The walls of the breakfast room (at the left of the main block) were hung with eleven Turner watercolours of lakes—Derwentwater, Constance, and several of Lucerne—and Goldau, St Gotthard, Schaffhausen, Coblentz and Llanthony. These were interspersed with 'doves by Hunt'.

The dining and drawing rooms—the rooms on the ground floor on either side of the front door—were large enough for their 'grandest receptions—never more than twelve for dinner'.[18] Here was more of their expanding picture collection: family portraits, with Turner's 'Slave Ship' and watercolours by Prout (4), Hunt (2), Roberts (2), and others in the dining room; and a Lewis, a Holland, a Tayler, a Stanfield, two Copley Fieldings, three Prouts and fifteen Turners in the drawing room (by 1852). On the floor above, on the west side, overlooking the drive, were Mr & Mrs Ruskin's rooms, with more Turners and family portraits by George and Thomas Richmond and G. F. Watts.

Above the morning room was Ruskin's study—about 15 feet × 20 feet and filled with work tables and bookcases—and above that his bedroom. The room on this second floor in the right-hand bay was where Ruskin kept his collection of minerals.

Below ground, the cellars were well stocked, as befitted a sherry importer who entertained frequently. John James listed the contents of his cellar on several occasions. In 1849, among other wines, there were 30 dozen Cockburn Port, bottled 1840 (£76) and 23 dozen Harris Port bottled 1830 (£115), 12 dozen Muscatel, 16 dozen pints and an octave (13½ gallons) of Paxarete, a sweet wine used in the blending of sherry, and 109 dozen bottles and a hogshead (54 gallons) of sherry. He noted the total value as £777 19s.—but 'if sold at public sale would bring a much greater price—they are too curious for general use.'[19] Ten years later he still had 14 dozen of the Harris 1830 Port left (now worth £117 12s.). In all in 1859 there were 79 dozen port and 64 dozen sherry in the cellar. Additionally he had 22½ dozen sherry (including 2½ dozen 'very old') which he sold to the Queen for £87 16s. Still remaining were 3½ dozen pints of Nelson sherry, sherry from the butt from which Admiral Lord Nelson was supplied shortly before Trafalgar, which John James prized highly and with which John's health was always toasted at his birthday dinners. Although the content of the cellar had changed in 1859 the value remained—to within £2—the same as ten years earlier.

The house was often filled with guests, either resident or for dinner. Dinner was usually at six, thus allowing the guests a view over the field and the Norwood hills in the evening light. And what guests there were too! The list is a roll call of Victorian literary and artistic life—J. D. Harding, Joseph Severn, Tom and George Richmond, J. M. W. Turner, G. F. Watts, Millais, Woolner, W. B. Scott, Dante and William Rossetti, Holman Hunt, Leighton, Coventry Patmore, F. J. Furnivall, W. H. Harrison, Charles Newton, William Morris, Edward Burne-Jones, the Brownings, Henry James, Charles Kingsley; Carlyle often rode over from Cheyne Walk on Fritz, Tennyson came to see the Turners, Octavia Hill to talk about housing reform and to glean the germ of an idea for the National Trust. Ruskin's birthday on 8 February was always a special day in the household, with an extra special dinner. In 1848 for instance there was Turner,

10 No. 163 Denmark Hill

11 No. 163 Denmark Hill, back view

Boxall, Richmond, Eastlake and Rev Daniel Moore; 1860 saw the two Richmonds, two Rossettis, Harrison and Furnivall as guests.

To run the house and garden, and to attend to the needs and comfort of their guests, John James Ruskin employed six female staff and his son's manservant in 1843. The number of indoor staff remained fairly constant, with an outdoor staff of three or four gardeners. Arthur Severn says in his *Memoir of Ruskin* that by 1871 Ruskin employed seven gardeners at Denmark Hill. In a different category was George Allen. He became Ruskin's full-time assistant in 1857, having married Anne Hobbs, Mrs Ruskin's maid, in the previous year. They lived at the lodge—perhaps from their marriage; they were certainly there in 1862.

The gardens were probably overseen by Margaret Ruskin, who had enjoyed working in the Herne Hill garden. As she grew older, no doubt Ruskin himself took a hand. After his father's death in 1864, he told Lady Trevelyan that he had instructed his gardeners to grow all sorts of old English flowers, with wild roses all round the garden. He had ordered the planting of twenty peach and almond trees alternately along the walk where they would catch the spring sunsets.

> I pay £50 a year ground rent, and £250 a year in wages to my gardeners; besides expenses in fuel for hothouses, and the like. And for this sum of £300 odd pounds a year I have some pease and strawberries in summer, some camellias and azaleas in winter; and good cream, and a quiet place to walk in all the year round . . . The camellias and azaleas stand in the anteroom of my library; and everybody says, when they come in, 'How pretty!' and my young lady friends have leave to gather what they like to put in their hair, when they are going to balls'.[20]

Margaret Ruskin died on 5 December 1871 and Ruskin sold 163 Denmark Hill to Walter Druce. The house had never really been 'home' to him, but he did confess to an apprehensiveness at the prospect of leaving it. On 28 March 1872 he wrote in his diary 'Thursday morning. Denmark Hill. Last day. I write my morning date for the last time in my old study'.[21] He went to Oxford, and on the next day, Good Friday, wrote 'In my college rooms, having finally left my old home'. Eighteen months later he wrote from Brantwood to Charles Norton, 'I am happier than I was at Denmark Hill—and yet look back to Denmark Hill, enraged at myself for not knowing its blessings'.[22]

Most of Ruskin's most important books, *Modern Painters, Seven Lamps of Architecture, Stones of Venice,* the earlier volumes of lectures, *Political Economy of Art, Sesame and Lilies, Crown of Wild Olive,* and *Unto this Last,* were mainly written at Denmark Hill, for even during his married life most of his literary work was done in the study at 163 Denmark Hill.

The house on Denmark Hill was to see many changes. Many alterations and additions were made. Later it was amalgamated with the large house and grounds next door which from 1863 had belonged to

Sir Henry Bessemer, inventor of the steel process which bears his name. It became a large hotel, known as Ruskin Manor, with golf course and tennis club. The whole flourished for many years, but was finally demolished in 1947 to make way for a huge London County Council housing estate.

12 Effie Ruskin

4 No. 30 Herne Hill

John's unsuccessful marriage began in 1848. For the first three and a half years John and Effie had no real home of their own; their base was at 163 Denmark Hill. However, they travelled a lot, particularly spending long periods of time in Venice while Ruskin assembled material for his book, *The Stones of Venice*. For a while, when they were in England in 1850–51, they took the lease of a house in Park Street, Mayfair, but this was given up when they returned to Venice in the summer of 1851.

Not until December 1851 were plans for the young Ruskins' eventual home under discussion between father and son. Ruskin needed somewhere quiet and so the house could not be in London. John James looked at several houses for John, and eventually heard that No. 30 Herne Hill, the adjacent house to semi-detached 28 Herne Hill, was available.

John James described the house to his son.

> Your Herne Hill House is a most convenient one and I hope will please—the principal Bedroom commands a far wider prospect than this house [Denmark Hill] & is so cheerful I fear I should never rise to Breakfast. The Dining Room is better lighted than here & would take 16 or 20 people. Your study and adjoining Dressing Room have large windows to *East* & *West*. Under you George [Ruskin's valet] has Bedroom & front working—Daguerreotype—or work of any kind Room and behind a Lumber Room—Drawing Room very pretty. Two excellent little cellars—water now laid on from Kingston & water from wells in Kitchen . . .[23]

After negotiations, John James Ruskin bought the 34-year lease for £1300 17s 8d. Snell of Albemarle Street, the house furnishers whom the Ruskins patronised, were given *carte blanche* with the furnishing and knocked two rooms into one for John's study—at a further cost of £2327 10s.

The furnishings were a bone of contention. Effie Ruskin told her brother that John was furious and said the house was only fit for a clerk to live in, and he would be ashamed to invite his friends there. Effie herself said that 'I found what I expected, viz, that Mr R had given Mr Snell a large sum of money to do up the House—which Mr Snell had naturally done up as cheaply and vulgarly as he could and put half the money in his pocket . . '[24]

Despite his enlarged study, on most days John walked down to 163 Denmark Hill to his study there. This Herne Hill house was not occupied for very long. For most of the season of 1853 the Ruskins took rooms in Charles Street, Mayfair, later taking a long holiday with the Millais brothers in Scotland. The Ruskins' marriage eventually broke down and they left 30 Herne Hill in April 1854.

No doubt some of the furniture was moved to Denmark Hill; certainly nearly £800 worth was sold back to Snell. The house itself was retained and let to a Mr J. Cole for £130 p.a.

John James Ruskin still owned the lease at his death in 1864 and it was inherited by John. It had been an unhappy house but a sound investment. Of the initial 1852 investment of £3528 7s 8d, some furniture and £2060 19s 3d had been recovered by 1864. It is not clear when John sold the lease, but if he retained it until it expired, letting it at the same rate, it would have shown a profit of £1392 11s 7d.

5 Friends and Neighbours

In a typically Victorian way, John James and Margaret Ruskin found it difficult to mix with those in classes socially above or beneath them. When travelling on business John James always took the *second* best room in an hotel in case one of his customers or a member of the nobility should come and require accommodation. His servants, though treated with great kindness and consideration, were nevertheless servants. His letters to George Allen (his son's assistant but destined to become his publisher and only source of income in his old age) are written in the third person. This attitude of his parents perhaps created in Ruskin a slightly snobbish person who, although he mixed quite happily with royalty and crossing sweepers, nevertheless wrote slightly disparagingly of their London tradesmen neighbours—overlooking for the while that his father was only 'an entirely honest merchant'.

Thus in John James's diary,[25] where he usually recorded the names of visitors to his home, we see that among the most frequent were old friends from Scotland, members of the wine trade, local clergy, his physician Dr Grant with his wife and stepdaughters the Misses Sidney, and W. H. Harrison. Sometimes JJR's clerks came to dinner—Watson and Ritchie—and sometimes his partner Pedro Domecq came to stay, or his family, Count and Countess Bethune, Count and Countess Chabrillan, or Count and Countess Maison. Their other visitors were largely John's friends and drawn from all classes—Oxford friends such as Lord Athlone or Lord Eastnor (John's sponsor at Court), and of course the literary and artistic worthies of the day.

One of these, Samuel Prout, lived close by at 5 De Crespigny Terrace from 1845 until his death in 1852. The Ruskins seem to have had no social contact with Sir Henry Bessemer, their next-door neighbour from 1863. One of the most frequent callers at Herne Hill and Denmark Hill was W. H. Harrison, who lived at 2 Langport Place, in the New Road area of Camberwell Green. Harrison worked in the Crown Life Office in Bridge Street and was Registrar of the Royal Literary Fund. After the death in 1834 of Thomas Pringle, Harrison became the editor of *Friendship's Offering,* an appointment which he held until 1841. During this time, and after, many of Ruskin's poems were published in *Friendship's Offering,* and Harrison helped polish Ruskin's literary manuscripts before they were finally published. Ruskin described him as his 'literary godfather'.

Richard Gray was a friend of JJR's youth. They had met about 1815 when JJR was learning the sherry trade in Jerez, Cadiz and Lisbon and Richard Gray was with a Spanish house in Lisbon. The friendship was long-lasting and when Gray married and returned to England he settled near the Ruskins at 2 Grove Hill Terrace, Camberwell. The Grays often dined at the Ruskins', but while Margaret and John frequently dropped in at 2 Grove Hill Terrace, this friendly casualness does not seem to have happened in reverse.

Thomas Griffith, a picture dealer and from about 1841 Turner's agent, lived nearby at Hill House, Crown Lane, Norwood. In 1845 he opened a gallery in Pall Mall, but, as Andrew Wilton observes, he was perhaps too gentlemanly to be described as a dealer. Although JJR bought a number of Turner watercolours from him, he did not like him, and Griffith never appears to have dined at Denmark Hill or Herne Hill. But John often visited Griffith—indeed it was at Griffith's house where he first met Turner—and he wrote to his father of Griffith, 'I have an affection for him—having passed many happy hours in his Norwood house, and having got through him, all that I most value in the world'.[26]

Elhanan Bicknell was another customer of Griffith. He started collecting Turners in the early 1840s, just a little later than the Ruskins and he built up a collection of ten oils including Port Ruysdaal and Campo Santo, Venice (this latter when painted was one of the two most beautiful pieces of colour by Turner that Ruskin knew)—and fourteen watercolours including the Blue Righi, Lake Lucerne and Calder Abbey, Cumberland. Bicknell was the proprietor of a whaling fleet and his large house was just across the road from 28 Herne Hill. Ruskin and Bicknell were certainly on visiting terms because in his 1878 *Turner Catalogue,* Ruskin described the position of the Blue Righi in Bicknell's house—in his drawing room next to the window and opposite another Turner which was next to the door.

Edmund Oldfield, second son of Thomas Brame Oldfield of Champion Hill (a mile north east of Herne Hill but bordering the back of the Denmark Hill grounds), was one of Ruskin's earliest friends. They went to the Rev. Thomas Dale's school together. But Oldfield was two years older than Ruskin and he graduated from Worcester College, Oxford in 1837, the year in which Ruskin went up to Christ Church. Later, of course, they collaborated in the designs for the St Giles window. Oldfield became a barrister in the Inner Temple.

But the closest friend of Ruskin's early years was Richard Fall. The Falls—Richard and Eliza—lived four doors away from the Ruskins on Herne Hill—but John and Richard did not go to school together. Fall had a more formal education at Shrewsbury between 1834 and 1837. However, before he went away to Shrewsbury, and later during the holidays, they often enjoyed each other's company.

Richard Fall would come to Herne Hill and the mornings would be spent on the top floor in John's room, reading or writing. Then in the afternoon they would walk with their dogs. Fall was as fond of dogs as was Ruskin and in an early letter to his father Ruskin told him, 'Master Fall was pulling him [Dash] by the ears in the middle of the road yesterday to kiss him . . .'[27] When Ruskin was on the continent he wrote an important rhyming account of his tour through France to Fall, and later, in another rhyming letter, he told him about Oxford. In the holidays they went together to meetings of the Geological Society and in 1841 they embarked, in company with Ruskin's man George, on Ruskin's first tour independent of his parents. The tour took them to Wales and Ruskin has left an account of a ride which he took—'The only occasion in all my life on which I ever arrived at terms of amity and mutual understanding with a horse'.[28] But the tour was cut short because John had to return to Leamington Spa and the care of Dr Jephson.

Later, in 1849, Ruskin took Fall on a journey into the Alps when Ruskin introduced him to his favourite places and they enjoyed walks in the snow which reminded them of their youth. 'It was the last of our winter walks together'. Fall joined a mercantile firm, 'married a wife, very nice and pretty . . , held a rich man's faith in political economy; and bought bad prints of clipper packets in green sea; and so we gradually gave each other up—with all good wishes on both sides.' Richard Fall, who in 1856 was living on Denmark Hill, died at the age of 56 in 1878.

His sister Eliza 'an entirely worthy and unworldly girl' often called at the Ruskins', and became a firm friend of Ruskin's mother. They spent a lot of time together in Margaret's later years, and she also helped Ruskin as a copyist. After Margaret Ruskin's death, Eliza, who had inherited the family house at Herne Hill, gave it up and, Ruskin wrote in *Praeterita*, 'the last time I saw her she was enjoying some sort of town life in New Bond Street'. She died in 1881.

The Ruskins did not have a large circle of local friends, but they maintained a regular contact with this small number.

13 Beresford Chapel, 1824

14a Beresford Chapel, interior

14b Sketch of pulpit by Edward Burne-Jones

6 Beresford Chapel and the Rev. E. Andrews

The parish church when the Ruskins moved to Herne Hill would have been St Giles, Camberwell. However, from the early 1820s, when Ruskin was about four years old, instead of attending there on a Sunday they travelled down Herne Hill, Denmark Hill, and Camberwell Road to Beresford Street.

As Ruskin later related in *Praeterita*,[29]

> It began now to be of some importance what church I went to on Sunday morning. My father, who was still much broken in health, could not go to the long Church of England service, and, my mother being evangelical, he went contentedly, or at least submissively, with her and me to Beresford Chapel, Walworth, where the Rev. E. Andrews preached, regularly, a somewhat eloquent, forcible, and ingenious sermon, not tiresome to hear:—the prayers were abridged from the Church Service, and we, being the grandest people in the congregation, were allowed—though as I now remember, not without offended and reproachful glances from the more conscientious worshippers—to come in when even those short prayers were half over. Mary and I used each to write an abstract of the sermon in the afternoon, to please ourselves,—Mary dutifully, and I to show how well I could do it.

The Beresford Street Chapel was built in 1818, as the tablet in J. Hassell's 1824 watercolour shows. Ruskin described it elsewhere in his autobiography:[30]

> . . . Dr Andrews's was the Londonian chapel in its perfect type, definable as accurately as a Roman basilica,—an oblong, flat-ceiled barn, lighted by windows with semi-circular heads, brick-arched, filled by small-paned glass held by iron bars, like fine threaded halves of cobwebs; galleries propped on iron pipes, up both sides; pews, well shut in, each of them, by partitions of plain deal, and neatly brass-latched deal doors, filling the barn floor, all but its two lateral straw-matted passages; pulpit, sublimely isolated, central from sides and clear of altar rails at end; a stout, four-legged box of well-grained wainscot, high as the level of front galleries, and decorated with a cushion of crimson velvet, padded six inches thick, with gold tassels at the corners; which was a great resource to me when I tired of the sermon, because I liked watching the rich colour of the folds and creases that came in it when the clergyman thumped it.
>
> Imagine the change between one Sunday and the next, from the morning service in this building, attended by the families of the small shopkeepers of the Walworth Road, in their Sunday trimmings; (our plumber's wife, fat, good, sensible Mrs Goad, sat in the next pew in front of us, sternly sensitive to the interruption of her devotion by our late arrivals); fancy the change from this, to high mass in Rouen Cathedral, its nave filled by the white-capped peasantry of half Normandy!

Edward Andrews (d. 1841) was a good preacher and a very popular clergyman and the Ruskins probably continued to attend the Beresford Chapel while he remained there. There was soon to be an added connection with Dr Andrews. By 1829, thrice weekly young John Ruskin attended Dr Andrews's school, one of several in 'tutorial Walworth' as Ruskin was later to call it. Other than his parents, Andrews was Ruskin's first tutor, teaching him Hebrew and the Classics. Ruskin had also to write paraphrases of Andrews's sermons, as part of his lessons.

There were later coincidental connections with Dr Andrews and the Beresford Chapel. Andrews's daughter married Coventry Patmore, a friend of the adult Ruskin, who was instrumental in arranging Ruskin's initial support of the Pre-Raphaelite movement. And when *Praeterita* was published, Edward Burne-Jones wrote enthusiastically to Ruskin telling him that he too, as a boy, but after Andrews's time, had attended the Beresford Chapel. His sketch of the three-decker pulpit[31] makes an interesting accompaniment to Yates's 1825 watercolour of the chapel interior and Ruskin's description of it.

Beresford Street has now been re-named John Ruskin Street, but the Beresford Chapel still stands, hard by a railway bridge carrying the line from Herne Hill to the Elephant and Castle. Since it stopped being a chapel it has served as a garage, a tyre depot, a rag and scrap metal store, and a secondhand furniture warehouse. It is now sadly derelict and used as a centre for German sports cars.

15 Beresford Chapel, 1989

7 Rev. Thomas Dale's School in Grove Lane

In *Praeterita*[32] Ruskin explains that

> . . . it having been perceived by my father that Dr Andrews could neither prepare me for the University, nor for the duties of a bishopric, I was sent as a day scholar to the private school kept by the Rev. Thomas Dale, in Grove Lane, within walking distance of Herne Hill. Walking down with my father after breakfast, carrying my blue bag of books, I came home to half-past one dinner, and prepared my lessons in the evening for the next day.

Thomas Dale (1797–1870) graduated from Cambridge in 1822. From 1828 to 1830 he had been a professor of English literature and language at the University of London. In 1830 he came to Denmark Hill as the incumbent of St Matthew's Chapel, living in Grove Lane, which runs behind and parallel to Denmark Hill. In 1835 he became resident vicar of St Bride's, Fleet Street, and a year later, professor of English at King's College, London. 1843 saw his appointment to a Canonry of St Paul's, and from 1846 to 1861 he was vicar of St Pancras. He died in 1870 shortly after being appointed Dean of Rochester.

John James Ruskin's accounts record a first payment in December 1834 of £50 for a half year's tuition for John. Payments continued until December 1836.

Writing in *Fiction, Fair and Foul,*[33] Ruskin remembered that,

> on the first day when I went to take my seat in Mr Dale's schoolroom, I carried my old grammar to him, in a modest pride, expecting some encouragement and honour for the accuracy with which I could repeat, on demand, some hundred and sixty close-printed pages of it. But Mr Dale threw it back to me with a fierce bang upon his desk, saying (with accent and look of seven-times-heated scorn), 'That's a Scotch thing'.

The Latin Grammar, from which his mother had been teaching him, was that by Alexander Adam, rector of Edinburgh High School. No doubt Ruskin's father had used an earlier edition in his own education.

At Mr Dale's Academy in Grove Lane, Ruskin's fellow students were Willoughby Jones, son of Sir John Thomas Jones, and Kingsmill Grove Key who lived in nearby De Crespigny Terrace and whose father was twice Lord Mayor of London. The three sons of Colonel Matson of Woolwich were boarders. Additionally Dale taught his own three sons, Thomas, James and Lawford. Since Dale apparently moved to St Bride's in 1835 but continued to feature in John James's accounts until the end of 1836, presumably Ruskin must have trav-

16 Grove Lane, c. 1820

elled into London to pursue his education after 1835. In 1836 Ruskin attended Dale's lectures on early English literature at King's College.

Writing to JJR on Boxing Day 1836 Dale drew attention to Ruskin's deficiencies in Greek and Latin vocabulary, and an 'ignorance of grammatical niceties'. However, Dale pointed him in the right direction and 'he will do as well as though he had been educated at Eton or Harrow, provided only that he reads steadily . . . '[34]

Ruskin and Dale were to remain friends for many years and the Ruskins periodically attended Dale's services at St Bride's.

Ruskin's library contained a copy of Dale's *A Memorial of Pastoral Ministrations; Sermons, principally on points of Christian Experience, delivered in St Matthew's Chapel, Denmark Hill.* This little volume was printed at the expense of the congregation in 1836, for private circulation. With the exception of a very small number of copies, the whole edition was subscribed for.

About 1831, and until at least 1835, Ruskin also had lessons from Mr Rowbotham, who with his wife kept a young gentlemen's academy near the Elephant and Castle ('still in that unlucky Walworth'). Rowbotham was engaged to teach Ruskin mathematics; he also appears to have taught him French and Geography.

In *Praeterita*[35] Ruskin said that he 'went easily through the first three books of Euclid, and got as far as quadratics in Algebra. But there I stopped virtually for ever'—clearly an exaggeration for he went on to read Classics and Mathematics at Oxford and obtained a Double Fourth.

No doubt in the four years that he was taught by Rowbotham, Ruskin journeyed to the house near the Elephant and Castle, 'one of the first houses which have black plots of grass in front, fenced by iron railings from the Walworth Road', but in *Praeterita* he wrote of Rowbotham coming out to Herne Hill twice a week in the evenings. Rowbotham was always invited to a substantial tea 'with us before the lesson as a really efficient help to his hungry science, after the walk up Herne Hill, painful to asthma'.

8 Camden Chapel

Various writers, not the least Ruskin himself, have suggested that the family began to attend the Camden Chapel in Peckham Road as being more fitting to their more elevated station, acquired with their new house on Denmark Hill in 1843. However, the Ruskin familiy letters show that John James Ruskin attended there at least once in 1839.

Some time before 1841 they had begun attending St Bride's in Fleet Street, following Ruskin's tutor, Thomas Dale there. Ruskin tells us in *Fiction Fair and Foul*[36] that when Dale moved from St Bride's to the parish of St Pancras, they began to go to Camden Chapel.

Here the minister was another evangelical and well-respected preacher, the Rev. Henry Melvill (1798–1871). It is clear that Margaret Ruskin approved of Melvill. 'We had a most instructive Sermon from Mr Melvill on Sunday', she wrote to her husband in June 1843,[37] 'proving most satisfactorily from the Text "whosoever denieth the Son the same hath not the Father" the divinity of Christ'.

This service must have been not long before Melvill moved from Camden Chapel to become the Principal of Haileybury College, an appointment which he held until 1857. Meanwhile in 1853 he was appointed a Chaplain to Queen Victoria. In 1856 he became a Canon of St Paul's, and from 1863 to 1871 he was Rector of Barnes.

Ruskin long remembered Melvill and there are occasional references to him in his diary many years later. In his autobiography[38] he wrote:

> The transition to Denmark Hill had, however, in the first pride of it, an advantage also in giving our family Puritanism, promotion to a distinguished pew in Camden Chapel, quite near the pulpit. Henry Melvill, afterwards Principal of Haileybury, was the only preacher I ever knew whose sermons were at once sincere, orthodox, and oratorical on Ciceronian principles. He wrote them from end to end with polished art, and read them admirably, in his own manner; by which, though the congregation affectionately expected it, they were always deeply impressed. He arranged his sermons under four or five heads, and brought each in its turn to a vigorously pointed climax, delivering the last words of each paragraph with two or three energetic nods of his head, as if he were hammering that much of the subject into the pulpit cushion with a round-headed mallet. Then all the congregation wiped their eyes, blew their noses, coughed the coughs they had choked over for the last quarter of an hour, and settled themselves to the more devoted acceptance of the next section . . . Henry Melvill . . . dutifully forbidding himself any dangerous fields of inquiry, explained with accuracy all that was explicable in his text, and argued the inexplicable into the plausible with great zeal and feeling;—always thoroughly convincing himself before he attempted to convince his congregation. . . .For the rest, Mr Melvill was entirely amiable in the Church

> visitant, though not formidable in the Church militant. There were not many poor in the district to be visited; but he became at once a kindly and esteemed friend to us, as, for the present, serenely feeding lambs of his flock; and I shall always remember gratefully the unoffended smile with which one day, when he had called late, and I became restless during his conversation because my dinner was ready, he broke off his talk, and said, 'Go to your dinner'. I was greatly ashamed of myself for having been so rude; but went to my dinner,—[and] attended better to Mr Melvill's preaching ever afterwards . . .

Melvill was succeeded at Camden Chapel by the Rev. Daniel Moore, to whom Ruskin also seems to have been well-disposed. In 1851, when Ruskin and his wife were travelling to Venice, they were joined by Moore and his wife in Paris and they continued for two weeks together through Switzerland. Ruskin found Moore 'a most agreeable companion'.

17 Camden Chapel, c. 1870

In 1853 Moore set in motion plans for the enlargement of Camden Chapel. He was enthusiastic about the gothic style and although George Gilbert Scott had probably already been selected to design the extensions, Moore, knowing of Ruskin's friendship with Millais, was anxious to have the Pre-Raphaelites design a window. Unknown to Moore, Millais had already designed the tracery for a window head while at Glenfinlas with the Ruskins in the summer of 1853. In this design, the angels which form the tops of the arches all had faces modelled on Effie Ruskin's features. Millais seems to have sent this design to Moore. JJR, who had been sceptical about the possible Pre-Raphaelite involvement in the scheme, became very enthusiastic when he saw the design.

However, Effie's separation from Ruskin in the following year made the use of that design impractical, although as late as December 1854 Ruskin was asking Millais if he had given up all thought of architectural design.

Moore went ahead with his plans. Scott designed the extensions and Ruskin helped with the glass. He was very much involved in advising Moore on decoration and other features, particularly in relation to the decoration of pillars and the organ case. The new chancel followed Ruskin's architectural views closely, and he wrote to Moore, 'I think the design *faultless* and exceedingly beautiful'.

Cook and Wedderburn,[39] who sweepingly say that Ruskin added a chancel to the chapel with painted windows and sculptured pillars, add that the church was much damaged by fire in 1907. The Camden Chapel was finally destroyed during the second world war.

9 Camberwell Green

One of the delights of Ruskin's childhood was the pond on Camberwell Green. It was a landmark in his early travels from Herne Hill.

> My father would never drive with four horses in sight of his sober neighbours—the second pair were always sent on to wait at the foot of Greenwich Hill. But the fresh first pair used to trot down the hill and along the level of the Old Kent Road, and that first trot through Camberwell, the turn by the pond on the Green, which was going to lead one—in a week or so—to the lake of Geneva,—the sense of pity for the inhabitants of Peckham, who weren't going . . .[40]

But Ann Strachan, his nurse, always protected John from the pond's mysterious dangers.

18 Pond on Camberwell Green, c. 1820

. . . even between us [at Herne Hill] and tutorial Walworth there was one Elysian Field for me in the neglected grass of Camberwell Green. There *was* a pond in the corner of it, of considerable size, and unknown depth,—probably, even in summer, full three feet in the middle; the sable opacity of its waters adding to the mystery of danger. Large, as I said, for a pond, perhaps sixty or seventy yards the long way of the Green [north-south], fifty the short; while on its western edge grew a stately elm, from whose boughs, it was currently reported, and conscientiously believed, a wicked boy had fallen into the pond on Sunday, and forthwith the soul of him into a deeper and darker pool. It was one of the most valued privileges of my early life to be permitted by my nurse to contemplate this judicial pond with awe, from the other side of the way.[41]

In *Praeterita* Ruskin mourned the drainage of the pond. 'The loss of it, by the sanitary conversion of Camberwell Green into a bouquet for Camberwell's button-hole, is to this day matter of perennial lament to me.'[42]

19 Camberwell Green, 1989

10 Croxted Lane

Travel south to the end of Herne Hill. At the junction—at the Half Moon and Herne Hill Station—it becomes Norwood Road. Very soon, Croxted Road, or Croxted Lane, as it was—forks off to the left, about half a mile from 28 Herne Hill.

In his youth Ruskin often walked this way; '. . . what lovely hedges of [wild roses] there were in the lane leading from Dulwich College up to Gipsey Hill.' He frequently came to the Gallery at Dulwich to see the Old Masters, particularly when writing *Modern Painters*. As he explained in the Preface to the first volume, 'Whatever particular references have been made for illustration have been confirmed, as far as was in my power, to works in the National and Dulwich Galleries.'[43] He walked past the 'tadpole-haunted ditch in Croxted Lane' to see paintings at Dulwich and there are frequent references to works in this collection by Claude, Cuyp, Hobbema, Poussin, Rubens, Salvator Rosa and others in *Modern Painters*.

How different was Croxted Lane then.

> In my young days, Croxted Lane was a green bye-road traversable for some distance by carts; but rarely so traversed, and, for the most part, little else than a narrow strip of untilled field, separated by blackberry hedges from the better-cared-for meadows on each side of it: growing more weeds, therefore, than they, and perhaps in spring a primrose or two—white archangel-daisies plenty, and purple thistles in autumn. A slender rivulet, boasting little of its brightness, for there are no springs at Dulwich, yet fed purely enough by the rain and morning dew, here trickled—there loitered—through the long grass beneath the hedges, and expanded itself, where it might, into moderately clear and deep pools, in which, under their veils of duck-weed, a fresh-water shell or two, sundry curious little skipping shrimps, any quantity of tadpoles in their time, and even sometimes a tittlebat, offered themselves to my boyhood's pleased, and not inaccurate, observation. There, my mother and I used to gather the first buds of the hawthorn; and there, in after years, I used to walk in the summer shadows, as in a place wilder and sweeter than our garden, to think over any passages I wanted to make better than usual in *Modern Painters*.

Ruskin found his favourite walk sadly changed when he revisited it in 1880.

> On the first mild—or, at least, the first bright—day of March, in this year, I walked through what was once a country lane, between the hostelry of the Half-moon at the bottom of Herne Hill, and the secluded College of Dulwich . . . no existing terms of language known to me are enough to describe the forms of filth, and modes of ruin, that varied themselves along the course of Croxted Lane. The fields on each side of it are now mostly dug up for building, or cut through into gaunt corners and nooks of blind ground by the wild crossings and concurrencies of three railroads. Half a dozen

20 Croxted Lane, c. 1880

handfuls of new cottages, with Doric doors, are dropped about here and there among the gashed ground: the lane itself, now entirely grassless, is a deep-rutted, heavy-hillocked cart road, diverging gatelessly into various brickfields or pieces of waste; and bordered on each side by heaps of—Hades only knows what!—mixed dust of every unclean thing that can crumble in drought, and mildew of every unclean thing that can rot or rust in damp: ashes and rags, beer-bottles and old shoes, battered pans, smashed crockery, shreds of nameless clothes, door-sweepings, floor-sweepings, kitchen garbage, back-garden sewage, old iron, rotten timbers jagged with out-torn nails, cigar-ends, pipe-bowls, cinders, bones, and ordure, indescribable; and, variously kneaded into, sticking to, or fluttering foully here and there over all these, remnants, broadcast, of every manner of newspaper, advertisement or big-lettered bill, festering and flaunting out their last publicity in the pits of stinking dust and mortal slime.

The lane ends now where its prettiest windings once began; being cut off by a cross-road leading out of Dulwich to a minor railway station: and on the other side of this road, what was of old the daintiest intricacy of its solitude is changed into a straight, and evenly macadamised carriage drive between new houses of extreme respectability, with good attached gardens and offices—most of these tenements being larger—all more pretentious, and many, I imagine, held at greatly higher rent than my father's, tenanted for twenty years at Herne Hill.[44]

21 Croxted Road, 1989

11 St Giles Church

The old St Giles Church in Camberwell was built in 1152. North and south aisles were added in the 13th century, and the early 16th century saw a major reconstruction. The Ruskins would have known this church since they moved into the area, although they may never have worshipped there. The old church came to an end on 7 February 1841, the day before Ruskin's 22nd birthday. The faulty heating system caused a fire which was fuelled by the large amount of woodwork in the building. The destruction was almost total, although there are still a few relics which survived the fire.

Plans were immediately put in hand for the rebuilding of the church. The incumbent, the Rev. J. G. Storie, was apparently a go-ahead person and funds were soon raised (J. J. Ruskin gave £100 10s.) to supplement the considerable amount of insurance money that was available. As the outcome of a competition, George Gilbert Scott was appointed architect and he designed a large Transitional Gothic building, spacious enough to be in keeping with the needs and status of developing Camberwell. The new church, which stands at the point where Camberwell Church Street becomes Peckham Road, was opened in 1844.

Ruskin and his friend Edmund Oldfield—they had attended Thomas Dale's school together—both took a great interest in the rebuilding and furnishing of St Giles, and their interest took a practical form in the design of the east window. The original intention had been to have the window made by the London firm of Ward & Nixon. But Ruskin and Oldfield considered that Ward's designs were insufficiently medieval, and they determined to prepare their own designs. First, Ruskin prepared drawings for the window heads, but these too were insufficiently medieval, so new drawings were made by Oldfield which were ultimately used.

Next, Ruskin and Oldfield were asked to prepare designs for the five great lancets which form the principal part of the east window. In 1844 Ruskin travelled to Rouen and Chartres to study the glass there, and he gave much advice on the colours to be used. Oldfield, meanwhile, was left to oversee the making of the actual windows. It appears from the correspondence that Ruskin was happy to leave the actual designs to Oldfield, merely bombarding him with advice and information from France. 'I leave the choice entirely to Mr Storie and you; I mean, don't do a *single* thing out of complaisance to me, as I only wish to lay as much material before you as I can, to enable you to choose . . .'[45] But he did also send sketches for the window details.

The current guide to the church explains that the details of the design are 'intentionally indistinguishable from a distance in order not to distract the worshippers.'

22 *St Giles Church, 1826*

23 St Giles Church, east window, 1989

The window tells the Bible story. From left to right the lancets illustrate from the Creation to Moses; Exodus to Ahasuerus and Esther; Stoning of Stephen, Conversion of St Paul, and similar scenes; the fifth lancet contains scenes from the Apocalypse. In all there are sixty-nine different subjects, sixty-four patriarchs, apostles and New Testament figures.

The pamphlet, *A Description of a Painted Window in the Chancel of St Giles Church*, Camberwell (?1844), almost certainly written by Oldfield rather than by Ruskin himself, only describes the window heads and the central lancet, pointing out that the four lateral lights 'are for the present filled with white glass, the funds in the possession of the Committee appointed to superintend the undertaking not being adequate to the execution of a design for painting the entire window.' It is not clear when the outstanding four lights were completed.

During World War II the church suffered considerable damage. The east window particularly was badly damaged, but subsequently it was restored.

24 St Giles Church, 1989

25 St Paul's Church, interior, in the 1840s

12 St Paul's Church, Herne Hill

Across the road from 28 Herne Hill and a few hundred yards farther south, St Paul's Church was built by George Alexander, and opened in 1844. John James Ruskin obviously subscribed to the building of the new church as his accounts[46] show an entry in May 1843 for 'Herne Hill Church £105'. There are further donations: 'H. Hill Church £52 10s' in 1845, and 'Organ H. Hill £5' in March 1847. However, the church was not to Ruskin's taste and he perhaps regretted his father's generosity. Certainly he was pleased when in 1858 it was destroyed by fire.

The present, replacement, church was designed by G. E. Street, who until he opened his own practice in 1849 had worked with Scott, architect of the new St Giles, Camberwell.

Ruskin admired and supported Street's work—and in October 1858 his father supported the rebuilding of St Paul's with a donation of £100. In February of the following year Ruskin took the chair at a lecture delivered by Street to the Architectural Photographic Association. In his remarks from the chair Ruskin said that his

> 'neighours on Herne Hill had taken on themselves to build a Gothic church, which some two years ago was fortunately destroyed by fire. He immediately called on the different members of the congregation, and congratulated them on the occurrence. They thought him hard-hearted and lost to all feeling of true art; but since they had seen Mr Street's restoration of that church they admitted that he had been right all along.'[47]

Ruskin particularly admired the colouring of the bands of Devonshire marble in the piers of the nave and doubted that 'it could be excelled by any of the colours in ancient art'. In Ruskin's opinion, the new church was one of the loveliest of its kind in the country 'and one that makes the fire a matter of rejoicing'.

It was appropriate that there should be a memorial to Ruskin in the area where he spent so much of his life. Accordingly a memorial was placed on the north wall of the nave of St Paul's and was unveiled at a service in the evening of 8 February 1901, the day which would have seen his 82nd birthday.

Among those present at the ceremony were the Bishop of Southwark, the Mayor and Councillors of Camberwell, Alexander Wedderburn (one of Ruskin's literary trustees), and many others. Speaking after he had unveiled the memorial, Holman Hunt, the last surviving member of the Pre-Raphaelite Brotherhood, spoke of himself as one left alone after a great conflict for certain definite principles. Ruskin, Hunt said, had ever tried to spread the spirit of reverence. He had endeared himself by his private character, a man not only to be admired, but loved. The effect of *Modern Painters* was electrical; materialistic movements in art were transitory. Ruskin showed that art must have soul and mind. A memorial address was given by Professor H. C. Beeching.

The monument was designed in the Venetian Byzantine style by W. Brindley and the work was carried out by the firm of Farmer and Brindley. Arthur Severn gave some hints for the portrait medallion and Sir William Richmond also saw the drawings and made some useful suggestions.

The official history of the church describes the monument, which incorporates most of the important marbles used in St Mark's in Venice.

> It contains a portrait medallion of Ruskin sculptured in the Greek statuary of Pentelicus, on either side of which are panels in rose Giallo Antico, the whole under a canopy of white alabaster supported by columns of Verde Antico, from Thessaly, with carved capitals copied from those in the apse of the Duomo of Murano. Between these columns is an inscription panel of Rosso Antico, of Laconia, with letters in white enamel, and under this is a frieze of antique Cipollino marble, the whole being carried by a corbel carved with a Greek acanthus bossed in the centre to contain a circular plaque of Egyptian red porphyry, the same material as the grand columns on either side of the central portal of St Mark's. The Cipollino marble is that used for the 'incrustation' of the walls and great piers of St Mark's, the quarries of which are at Carystos, in Greece.

The wording on the memorial reads:

> John Ruskin, M.A., D.C.L, LL.D. Born in Bloomsbury, 8 Feb. 1819. Brought to 28 Herne Hill by his parents in 1823, he dwelt on Herne Hill and Denmark Hill for 50 years. His later days were chiefly spent upon the shores of Coniston Lake. Yet under the roof where he grew up he had a home in the Parish to the end, the house having passed into the possession of his cousin and adopted daughter, Joan, and her husband, Arthur Severn. Died at Brantwood, 20 Jan., buried at Coniston, 25 Jan. 1900. The words of the wise are as goads, and as nails well fastened are the words of the masters of assemblies.

The whole comes together to make what must surely be the most inappropriate Ruskin memorial imaginable!

26 St Paul's Church, 1989

13 John Ruskin and the Working Men's Institute, Camberwell

In 1853 John Ruskin, then a thoroughly well-established writer on art, was preparing to embark on a new career as lecturer. In the summer, in Scotland, he was preparing a series of lectures on architecture and painting; these he delivered in Edinburgh in the autumn. His parents were pleased at the reception his lectures received but were far from happy at the thought of their son being a lecturer. Indeed a guest at their dinner table had described being a lecturer as 'degrading'.

Thus, when Ruskin was invited to lecture in Camberwell the prospect upset his parents. 'I see small bills up through the village', wrote John James to him on 10 December 1953,[48] 'with all the lecturers' *names*—among them Mr White who gets your old clothes . . . you would by Camberwell lecture get approached by many neighbours whom neither you nor your wife would resist and soon find yourself in hot water . . .' Out of respect for his father's wishes, he didn't lecture, but did, later, accept the presidency of the Camberwell Working Men's Institute.

After his father's death in March 1864, Ruskin felt himself more free to develop his career as a lecturer and to pursue his growing interest in social and political economy. In December 1864 he delivered two lectures in Manchester which were later printed as *Sesame and Lilies;* then on 24 January 1865 he lectured to the Camberwell Working Men's Institute on 'Work and Play'.

Like the Working Men's College in London, where Ruskin had assumed responsibility for the art classes, the 'Institute' at Camberwell was an attempt to enlarge the scope of working-class education. The lectures were held in the Camberwell Hall, built in 1748, and still existing as 45 Grove Lane. It stands adjacent to the Grove Tavern in Camberwell Grove. The audience was probably not large, for as Ruskin wrote on 16 January to Miss Bell, 'The Camberwell lecture is not till tomorrow week and I am not sure even then if I could now keep tickets for you—for the room is very small and my neighbours are rather curious, having lately known and seen nothing of me.'[49]

The lecture was reported in *The Art Journal* and subsequently printed as 'Work' in the *Crown of Wild Olive,* a collection of Ruskin's lectures delivered at this time.

27 Camberwell Hall, 1989

14 Ruskin Park

The Camberwell which Ruskin knew as a small boy had changed dramatically by the end of the century. Further development was planned in 1904.[50] A large estate—Sanders' Estate—just across the road from 163 Denmark Hill, came onto the market and the intention was to use it for building development. Plans were approved, but when the nature of the development scheme became generally known there were objections, because this part of south London would be thus deprived of a beautiful and necessary open space.

A scheme was proposed, and put to the local authority in January 1905, that a little over 24 acres of the well-timbered estate, with a frontage of 1,050 feet onto Denmark Hill, should be purchased as a public park, in order to retain the great natural beauty of the area. By March the Parks Committee recommended that the Council should contribute £25,000 towards the purchase of the land.

In January 1906 negotiations for the purchase were successfully completed. The principal contributors to the purchase price were:

The London County Council	£25,000
Camberwell Metropolitan Borough Council	£10,000
Lambeth Metropolitan Borough Council	£ 5,000
Southwark Metropolitan Borough Council	£ 2,500
The City Parochial Foundation	£ 500

Additionally there were many private subscribers.

When the estate was taken over by the Council it comprised eight houses and their grounds, the principal one being Dane House. At this time, two were left standing. In the laying out of the grounds many difficulties had to be overcome, and where possible, existing trees were retained.

To honour his long association with the area, the new park was called Ruskin Park. It was formally opened, with much ceremony, by Evan Spicer, Chairman of the London County Council, on Saturday 2 February 1907.

Ruskin's name was not only perpetuated here. Just across the road, 163 Denmark Hill had become an hotel called Ruskin Manor by 1912. Elsewhere in London there were Ruskin Avenues, Roads, Walks, a Close, Gardens and a Ruskin Street. A Ruskin Gallery was named in his honour in 1902 in the South London Art Gallery, and Beresford Street, where there has been a major post-war development and where the Ruskins once went to hear the Rev. Edward Andrews preach, is now appropriately re-named John Ruskin Street.[51]

Notes

1 References to Ruskin's writings are given in the *Library Edition of the Works of John Ruskin,* edited by E. T. Cook and Alexander Wedderburn, London, 1903–12, 39 vols (hereafter referred to as *Works*), XXXV, 20. *Works* XXXV contains Ruskin's autobiography *Praeterita.* This has appeared in many editions and is currently available in an edition from Oxford University Press.
2 *Works* XXXV, 34.
3 *Works* XXXV, 36.
4 *Works* XXXV, 35.
5 Incorporated in the Ruskin Union Memorial Committee leaflet, 1900.
6 *Works* XXXV, 178.
7 *Works* XXVI, 275.
8 *Works* XXXV, 502.
9 *Works* XXXV, 39.
10 E. T. Cook: *Homes and Haunts of John Ruskin* (London 1912), 13.
11 *Works* XXXVII, 395.
12 Sheila Birkenhead: *Illustrious Friends* (London 1965), 367.
13 V. A. Burd (ed.): *Ruskin Family Letters* (Ithaca 1973, 2 vols), hereafter referred to as *RFL,* 690.
14 *RFL,* 684.
15 *RFL,* 691.
16 *Works* XXXV, 317–18.
17 *Works* XXXV, 317.
18 *Works* XXXV, 380.
19 John James Ruskin's Account Book, Ruskin Galleries, Bembridge School, Isle of Wight, Bem MS 29.
20 *Works* XXVII, 196.
21 John Ruskin's Diary, Bem MS 18.
22 *Works* XXXVII, 70.
23 John James Ruskin to John Ruskin, 24 Jan 1852, Bem L 4.
24 Mary Lutyens: *Millais and the Ruskins* (London 1967), 7–8.
25 Bem MS 33.
26 *Works* XIII, 478.
27 *RFL,* 259.
28 *Works* XXXV, 621.
29 *Works* XXXV, 71–2.
30 *Works* XXXV, 132–33.
31 Burne-Jones's memory of the pulpit was at fault and in his letter to Ruskin he sketched it the wrong way round. The original has been reversed in the present reproduction.
32 *Works* XXXV, 81–2.
33 *Works* XXXIV, 365.
34 Ruskin *did* read Greek and Latin steadily—throughout his life.
35 *Works* XXXV, 85.
36 *Works* XXXIV, 365.
37 *RFL,* 744.
38 *Works* XXXV, 386–87.
39 *Works* XXXVI, 201 n.
40 *Works* XXXV, 108 n.
41 *Works* XXXV, 89–90.

42 *Works* XXXV, 90.
43 *Works* III, 6.
44 *Works* XXXIV, 265 ff.
45 *Works* XII, 435 ff.
46 Bem MSS 28–29.
47 *Works* XVI, 462–63.
48 Bem L 4.
49 V. A. Burd (ed.): *The Winnington Letters* (London 1969), 535.
50 Many of the details in this section are taken from G. L. Gomme: *Opening of Ruskin Park, Denmark Hill, by Mr Evan Spicer, J.P., Chairman of the Council, on Saturday, 2nd February, 1907.* (London 1907).
51 There is another interesting connection between Ruskin and Camberwell, for there are close ties between Ruskin's Guild of St George and the Camberwell School of Art and Crafts. Until recently Mr Anthony Harris, the present Master of the Guild, was Head of the School, which is now a constituent college of The London Institute.

THE GUILD OF ST GEORGE

The Guild of St George was founded by John Ruskin in 1878. The Guild is a charitable Education Trust which receives applications for financial support from a wide variety of community projects. It also offers scholarships and awards across a range of subjects close to Ruskin's heart, including the practice of crafts and scholarly work in agricultural science and economics, art history, education, industry and the social sciences.

The Ruskin Lectures were inaugurated in 1978 to mark the centenary of the Guild. The following have been published as pamphlets:

Art and Society: Ruskin in Sheffield 1876 (1981) by Robert Hewison (£1.50)

Ruskin, Lady Mount-Temple and the Spiritualists: an episode in Broadlands history (1982) by Van Akin Burd (£1.80)

Why Have Our Little Girls Large Shoes? Ruskin and the Guild of St George (1985) by Anthony Harris, Master of the Guild (£2)

The Relevance of Ruskin (1988) by Sir Roy Shaw (£1.80)

The Guild has also published

Ruskin and Bewdley (1989) by Peter Wardle and Cedric Quayle (£2.95). A historical study to mark the centenary of a pioneer land settlement in Worcestershire.